JP

Monnier, Miriam

Just right

DUE DATE

10/02

Copyright © 2001 by Michael Neugebauer Verlag,
an imprint of Nord-Süd Verlag AG, Gossau Zürich, Switzerland.
First published in Switzerland under the title Ich bin ich.
English translation copyright © 2001 by North-South Books Inc.

All rights reserved. No part of this book may be reproduced or utilized in any form
or by any means, electronic or mechanical, including photocopying,
recording, or any information storage and retrieval system,
without permission in writing from the publisher.

First published in the United States, Great Britain, Canada,
Australia, and New Zealand in 2001 by North-South Books,
an imprint of Nord-Süd Verlag AG, Gossau Zürich, Switzerland.

Distributed in the United States by North-South Books Inc., New York.

Library of Congress Cataloging-in-Publication Data is available.
A CIP catalogue record for this book is available from The British Library.
ISBN 0-7358-1521-6 (trade binding) 10 9 8 7 6 5 4 3 2 1
ISBN 0-7358-1522-4 (library binding) 10 9 8 7 6 5 4 3 2 1
Printed in Germany

For more information about our books, and the authors and artists
who create them, visit our web site: www.northsouth.com

Miriam Monnier

Just Right!

Translated by
J. Alison James

A Michael Neugebauer Book
North-South Books
New York / London

This is me.
Sometimes I am big.
But sometimes I'm still little.
Actually I'm not exactly sure.

Mother says, "You are my big girl. You can climb
the stairs all by yourself."
But I still like her to carry me like a baby.

But then she says, "You can't have gum. You are much too little to chew it." But I can chew gum. I can make the loveliest long gum strings. I just can't blow bubbles yet.

When I eat with my fingers, Mother says, "You eat like
a baby. Use your fork like a big girl."
But it doesn't taste as good that way.

One day we went shopping and the shopkeeper said,
"You are such a big girl, helping your mother. Here,
have a lollipop." I liked that!
But Mother didn't.
She said, "Lollipops are
bad for your teeth."

After that I walked a little bit behind her so I could lick my lollipop in peace. But a lady came up and said, "You are too little to be out on your own. Where is your mother?"
All this was making me angry. Was I big or was I little? Everybody said something different.

At home, the boy downstairs was standing in his
doorway. When I asked him if he wanted to play,
he said "I can't play with you. You are too little!"
And he shut the door in my face.

I went home feeling sad and asked my mother if we could play robbers. But she said that she had lots of things to do and that I was a big girl and could play by myself.

That was it. I'd had enough. I stomped to my room,
slammed the door and threw myself on the bed.
I didn't want to hear another word.

Mother came in and asked me what was wrong. I began
to cry. "I don't know if I'm too big or too little!" I told her.

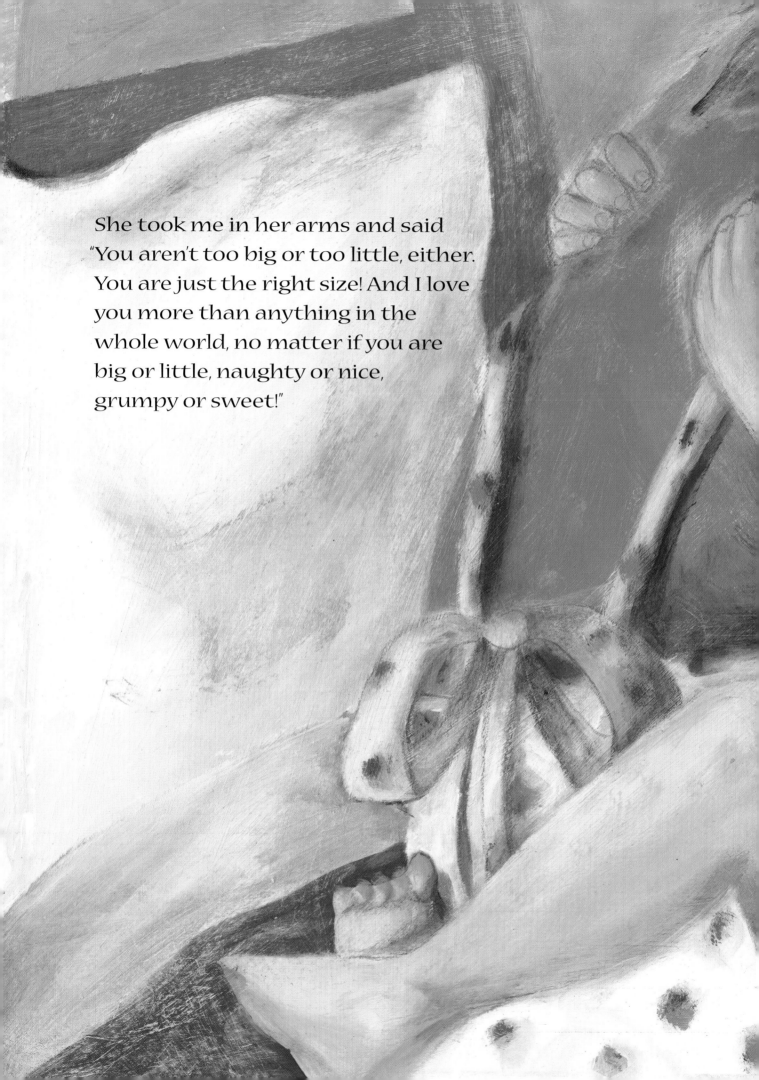

She took me in her arms and said
"You aren't too big or too little, either.
You are just the right size! And I love
you more than anything in the
whole world, no matter if you are
big or little, naughty or nice,
grumpy or sweet!"

The boy downstairs was waiting outside his door the next time we came home, but I didn't want to play with him. My mother and I held hands and went up the stairs together.